Dear mouse friends,
Welcome to the world of

Geronimo Stilton

THE RODENT'S GAZETTE
EDITORIAL STAFF

Geronimo Stilton
A learned and brainy mouse; editor of *The Rodent's Gazette*

Thea Stilton
Geronimo's sister and special correspondent at *The Rodent's Gazette*

Trap Stilton
An awful joker; Geronimo's cousin and owner of the store Cheap Junk for Less

Benjamin Stilton
A sweet and loving nine-year-old mouse; Geronimo's favorite nephew

Geronimo Stilton

MOUSE HOUSE HUNTER

Scholastic Inc.

Published by Scholastic Inc., 557 Broadway, New York, NY 10012. SCHOLASTIC and associated logos are trademarks and/or registered trademarks of Scholastic Inc.

ISBN 978-0-545-83554-1

Text by Geronimo Stilton
Original title *Geronimo cerca casa*
Cover by Giuseppe Ferrario (design) and Giulia Zaffaroni (color)
Illustrations by Danilo Loizedda (design) and Christian Aliprandi (color)
Graphics by Chiara Cebraro

Special thanks to AnnMarie Anderson
Translated by Julia Heim
Interior design by Kay Petronio

12 11 10 9 8 7 6 5 4 3 2 1 15 16 17 18 19

Printed in the U.S.A. 40
First printing 2015

Home Sweet Home

One winter morning, I woke up in **MY** cozy bed. Ah! How soft **MY** mattress was! And how nice to see the first *rays* of sunlight shining through the window of **MY** room.

I opened the window as I sipped hot tea from **MY** favorite mug. It was **cold** outside but so nice and warm in **MY** house.

Oh, excuse me! I **FORGOT** to introduce myself. My name is Stilton, Geronimo Stilton, and I run *The Rodent's Gazette*, the most famouse **newspaper** on Mouse Island.

As I was squeaking, I was listening to **MY** favorite **MUSIC** and eating breakfast in **MY** kitchen. In fact, I was stuffing my snout with cheese croissants. **Yum!**

I HAD BREAKFAST IN MY KITCHEN!

THEN I TOOK A SHOWER IN MY BATHROOM!

Then I took a **SHOWER** and brushed my teeth in **MY** bathroom before I headed into **MY** bedroom. There, I opened **MY** closet and picked out an **outfit** to wear.

Finally, I quickly but carefully dusted **MY** antique cheese rind collection, which I keep in a glass showcase in **MY** living room.

Ah, home sweet home!

I OPENED MY CLOSET AND PICKED OUT AN OUTFIT!

I DUSTED MY COLLECTION OF CHEESE RINDS!

HERE IS MY HOME SWEET HOME!

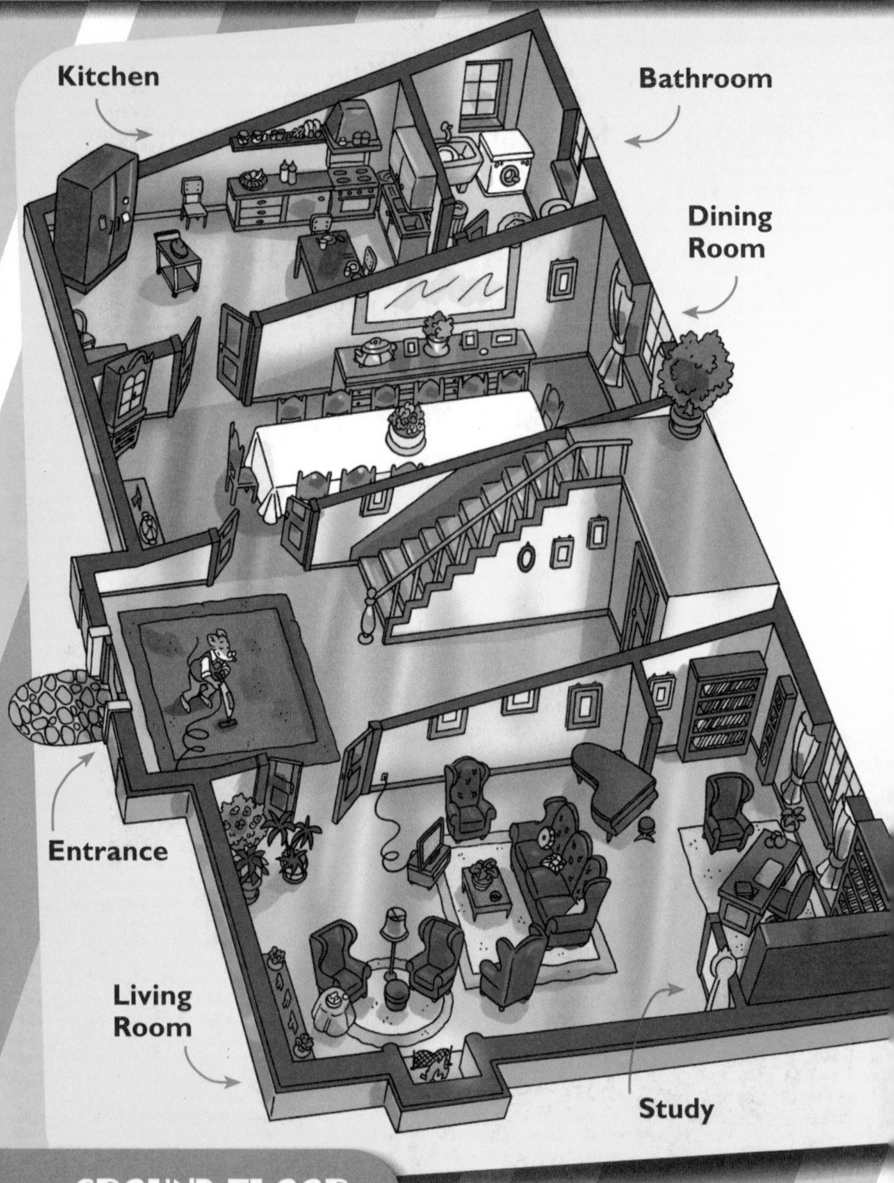

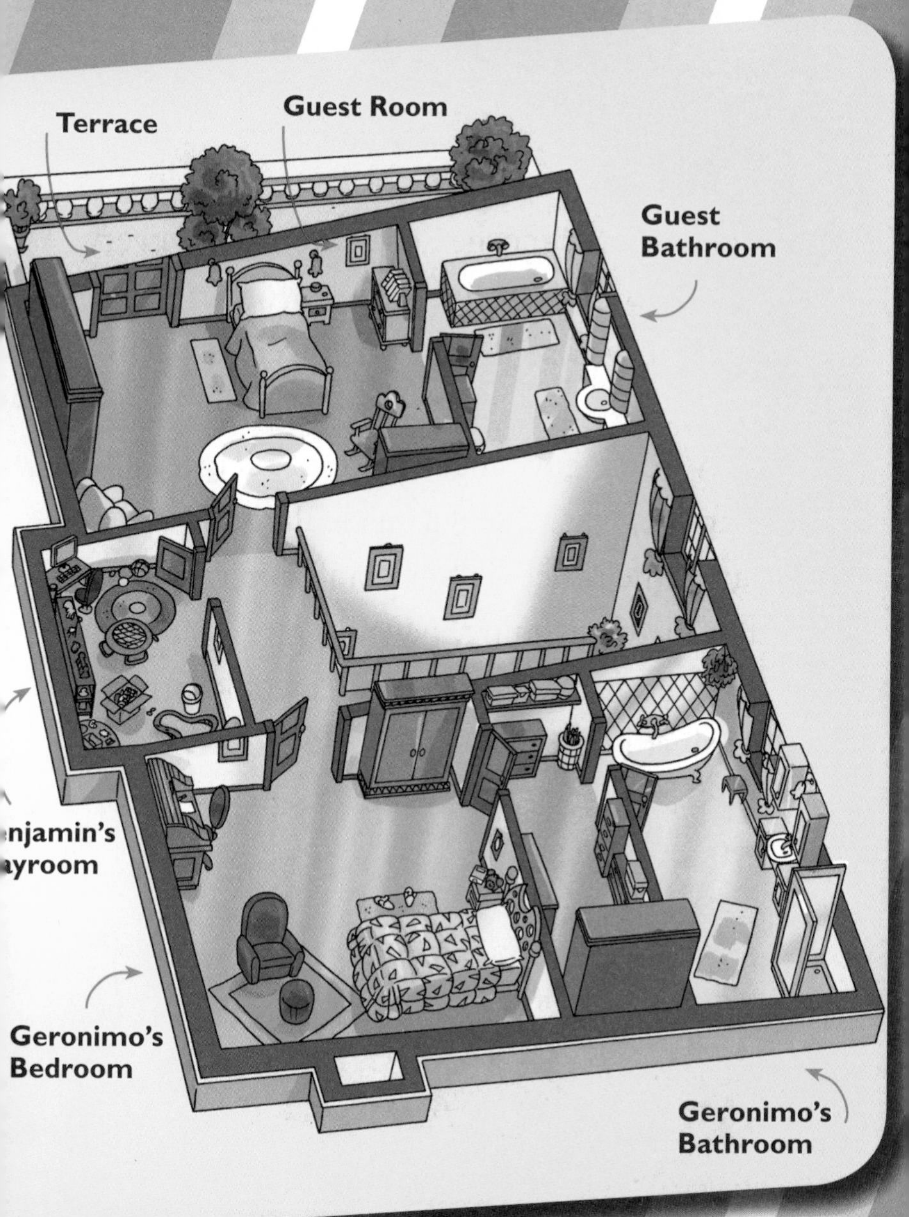

SECOND FLOOR

Oh, how I loved my house!

I knew every corner, every nook, and every DETAIL. I had lived there for so many years, it was as if the house were a part of **ME**.

My home gave me a sense of security. For example, when I had a particularly **HARD** day at the office, it was comforting to know that in the evening, I would **return** to **MY** home! There, the walls would protect me, just like **a turtle's shell**.

And whenever I'm on a dangerous or exciting adventure somewhere in the world, I always dream of coming home.

I've made so many **HAPPY** memories in my house over the years! From holidays to birthdays to special occasions — I've spent them all in my house, with my friends and family.

As I **dusted** my antique cheese rind collection that morning, I turned on the ***news***. I was stunned to see a reporter interviewing **Sally Ratmousen**, the editor of *The Daily Rat,* which is my newspaper's biggest **COMPETITOR**!

Moldy mozzarella! She seemed very pleased as she showed the reporter a copy of her newspaper.

"Can you **confirm** your story about the famouse newspaper *The Rodent's Gazette*?" the reporter asked. "Is it true that it's closing down? Are you **really** sure?"

Sally scowled. "Of course I'm sure!" she squeaked. "I'm super sure! Do I seem like the type of mouse who would publish **news** without checking the **FACTS** first? The manager of Ratley's Bank, **Ledger Moneymouse**, is my exclusive source!"

When Moneymouse **appeared** on the screen, he seemed slightly shorter and a little **CHUBBIER** than usual. **How strange!**

A Real Mouse Has to Make Sacrifices . . .

To my surprise, Moneymouse confirmed the story.

"I'm afraid it's TRUE!" he squeaked to the reporter. "It's very sad for *The Rodent's Gazette*, but we've just informed William Shortpaws that because of his grandson, Geronimo Stilton, *The Rodent's Gazette's* accounts are in the RED. The paper will have to **close**!"

Huh? What did he mean? How could the accounts be in the RED? And how was it **MY** fault? I had to find out what was going on right away. I really hoped Sally had ***invented*** the entire story to sell more copies of her newspaper!

And yet Moneymouse had confirmed the story . . . **how very strange**!

I said good-bye to my pet fish, **Hannibal**, and left the house at once. My whiskers **trembled** with anxiety as I headed toward 17 Swiss Cheese Center. As soon as I got to *The Rodent's Gazette*, I headed straight to my office.

Unfortunately for me, a mouse with short gray fur, **steel-rimmed** glasses, and a determined look on his snout was waiting for me there. It was my **GRANDFATHER**, William Shortpaws, who is also known as Cheap Mouse Willy. He confirmed the news in his own way . . .

"Grandson!" he **thundered**. "I have some **TERRIBLE** news. But don't worry — I'll **fix** everything!"

"How can you tell me not to **worry** if you're saying you have terrible news?!" I squeaked **anxiously**. "What is it?"

He put a paw on my shoulder and stared at me closely.

"This morning, Ledger Moneymouse called me and told me that we are short on money. *The Rodent's Gazette*'s account is in the **RED**! The newspaper is **bankrupt**! That means **HARD TIMES** are coming — I mean **REALLY, REALLY HARD**! We must all make sacrifices, especially you!"

"What?" I squeaked. "The account is in the **RED**? We're **BANKRUPT**? What **sacrifices**? And why **ME**?"

My grandfather continued. "**GRANDSON**,

when things get **DIFFICULT**, a real mouse knows how to make sacrifices for the common good. Are you a **real** mouse? Or are you just a silly-willy? Or a cheesebrain? Or a cheddarhead?"

"Of course I'm a **real** mouse!" I replied proudly. "I'm no silly-willy, or cheesebrain, or cheddarhead! "

Grandfather took out a handkerchief from his pocket and wiped a tear from his **EYE**.

"Grandson, this is very **SERIOUS**!" he squeaked. "*The Rodent's Gazette* is in danger of closing!"

"I'm sorry, Grandfather," I said. "I didn't know anything about it!"

I really hadn't known a **THING** about this crisis. **How strange!**

Suddenly, Grandfather began to sob.

"Geronimo, we're really in **TROUBLE**!" he said. "We might have to shut down at any moment! Think of your colleagues — they will be **jobless**!"

"W-well what can I do?" I stammered.

He clapped me on the shoulder with his paw.

"Well, you finally asked the RIGHT QUESTION!" he thundered, his eyes suddenly dry. "I guess you're not such a cheesehead after all! You see, Grandson, if you would just make a small sacrifice, then maybe everything might be okay!"

"But *what* is this small sacrifice I would have to make?" I asked, perplexed.

"It's simple," he replied. "You must SELL YOUR HOUSE. With the money you make, I can get *The Rodent's Gazette* back on its feet!"

"What?!" I yelled. "Sell my house? Cheese and crackers! But where will I live?"

"How can you be so SELFISH, Geronimo?" he barked. "Doesn't it matter to you that so many rodents will be out of a JOB? Doesn't it matter that *The Rodent's Gazette* — the newspaper that I founded — will be ruined? Huh? Huh? Huh?"

I was so confused! What did my HOUSE have to do with any of this?

"Please, let me think a second," I squeaked. "If it's really necessary that I make this sacrifice, then maybe . . . perhaps . . . I guess I will."

HE DRIED HIS TEARS ON MY SLEEVE!

THEN HE BLEW HIS NOSE ON MY TIE!

He dried his TEARS on my sleeve (How rude!), blew his nose on my new tie (How very rude!), and took my wallet out of my pocket (How very, very rude!).

"So, you'll sell your house to save the newspaper, then?" my grandfather asked.

"Y-yes, I will," I agreed reluctantly.

"GREAT!" my grandfather squeaked happily. "Meanwhile, if you don't mind, I'll keep all the money you have. I might need it for *The Rodent's Gazette.*"

HE TOOK MY WALLET OUT OF MY POCKET . . .

AND HE ALSO TOOK MY PEN AND MY GOLD WATCH!

Then he took from my pocket my gold watch (a gift from Aunt Sweetfur that I really cared about!) and my PLATINUM pen (a souvenir from the FIRST journalism contest I won!).

"And I'll take these things, too," he thundered. "I'm going to sell them to get some cash, if you don't mind."

I minded very much, but with tears in my eyes I agreed.

"Okay, Grandfather. If you need money to save *The Rodent's Gazette*, go ahead and take them.

Then Grandfather made me SIGN a piece of paper (I was so upset I didn't even ask why), before he left me alone in my office.

I was SAD. I was so, so sad — I was the saddest mouse in the world! The idea of going back home that night didn't make me feel good anymore, because soon it would no longer be MY HOME.

But somehow I gathered my strength. I had to go back to my house and get busy packing up my things and finding a place to stay.

As soon as I left my office and entered the newsroom, all of my colleagues at *The Rodent's Gazette* became very quiet.

"Oh, Geronimo, we heard the news," they muttered sadly. "We're so SORRY! It won't be easy for you! Thank you for the sacrifice you're making for us."

I gestured with my PAW as if to say, "It was nothing," but I couldn't utter those words. How could I say that it was okay even though my heart was breaking at having to sell the house that held my DEAREST memories?

Instead, I burst into TEARS.

We're so sorry!
Waaaaah!
Be strong!

Poor
Geronimo!

Good-bye, Mr. Stilton!

I gathered my strength and left *The Rodent's Gazette* with my spirits low but my snout high. I would get through this!

Then I headed home. The **florist** on the corner ran to meet me and offered me a rose with tears in her eyes.

"This is for you," she said. "You are a **kind** and sensitive rodent, which is so rare these days! I'm sorry to hear the **sad news**!"

I began to sob, and we cried for a while together. But then I had to stop because my **bus** was coming.

Three stops later, I got off in front of my house. As the bus pulled away, the driver turned and yelled: "I'll be sorry not to see you every morning! Good-bye, Mr. Stilton!"

When I arrived in front of my favorite

pastry shop, the baker ran out and offered me a FREE pastry.

"I heard you are moving away." he squeaked sadly. "I'm so sorry. Here's one last hot cheesy pastry before you go . . . Good-bye."

Finally, I arrived at home. I was about to open the front door when someone slapped me on the back and flicked my ear.

"So, have you sold the shack yet?" someone squeaked. "Do you have the cash? Come on, Grandfather is in a hurry!"

It was my cousin Trap. Do you know him? No? Lucky you!

"Trap, I haven't had time to SELL it yet," I muttered, still feeling so sad.

"Don't worry!" he said. "I'll take care of it!"

"You?!" I protested. "I didn't

know you were a real estate agent."

"I'm not," he squeaked. "But I am the best PROBLEM SOLVER in New Mouse City! I can do it all! And when I say all, I really mean EVERYTHING! I'll sell this SHACK for you in no time."

Then he opened an enormouse suitcase.

"Check it out, Cuz: Here's all my problem-solver equipment! Take a GAZE and be AMAZED!"

PROBLEM-SOLVER SUITCASE
Down jacket and pants for winter problems
Reinforced gloves for thorny problems
Sneakers to help get places quickly
Pocket planner
Business cards
Computer
Camera
Compass
Binoculars to examine the situation from afar
Magnifying glass to examine the situation up close
Portable refrigerator with extra food
Instant ice pack
Portable air conditioner
A fan to refresh ide
Tool belt
Gardening kit to solve problems from the roots up
Hammer t beat dow difficult problems
Measuring tape to size up big problem

THIS IS — I MEAN WAS — MY HOME!

I was confused: How would all that stuff help Trap sell my house?

"Well, if you feel up for it, and you're really sure you can do it, that's fine with me," I told my cousin. "I suppose someone has to do it, and maybe it's better if it's a relative. Maybe that will make it easier for me to give it up . . ."

SIGH! SNIFF, SNIFF.

I took a moment to blow my nose and dry my tears. Once I had composed myself, I continued.

"Listen, Trap," I told my cousin. "This is a very IMPORTANT job. Try to sell it for the best price you can. I have to save *The*

TRAP LOOKED AT THE ROOF . . .

HE EXAMINED THE WALLS OF THE HOUSE . . .

Rodent's Gazette — and everyone's **JOBS**!"

"Well, let me take a look around," Trap replied. "I'll **see** how much we can get for this place!"

He **GRABBED** his binoculars and examined the **roof**.

"Hmm . . . this roof definitely isn't NEW. Look, you can see that it needs to be redone."

He **tapped** the exterior walls with his hammer and squeaked, "Hmm . . . this house is very **old**. See these cracks here? That's bad! And that gutter is about to collapse!"

He examined the dirt and flowers in my garden.

"Look at this sad little thing!" he muttered. "This GARDEN needs help."

Then he went inside and dashed from one ROOM to another, peering at everything with his MAGNIFYING glass and huffing and sighing.

"This furniture is nothing SPECIAL," he

TRAP EXAMINED THE DIRT . . .

HE STUDIED THE FURNITURE . . .

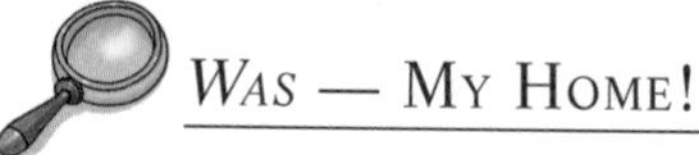

squeaked. "And these fixtures are ancient!

"The only thing valuable in this house is your collection of antique cheese rinds from the 1700s," Trap grumbled. "That's definitely worth something!"

"Oh, no you don't!" I said quickly. "My cheese rinds are not included with the house. They are my private, personal collection, and I'm taking them with me!"

Trap began snapping lots of PHOTOS.

Click!

"I'll do my best, Cuz, but this place is in bad shape," he said.

Click! Click!

"I don't think we'll get much for this sad little shack."

"How dare you!" I squeaked, exasperated. "It's not a shack! This is — I mean, *was* — my home!"

Please Hold . . .

I burst into TEARS.

"Come on now, Cousin, why are you crying?" Trap asked. "Do you want to SELL this house or not?"

I explained that I really didn't want to sell my house, but I had to! *The Rodent's Gazette* was in TROUBLE, and I had promised Grandfather I would help.

"I'm sorry about your house, Geronimo, but if you need to do it, just do it!" Trap advised me. "I'll HELP you, but the sooner we do it, the better, don't you agree?"

As much as I hated to admit it, I knew Trap was right. I might as well sell the house QUICKLY and try to move on.

At that moment, my cell phone RANG.

"So, have you sold the house yet?" my grandfather squeaked anxiously. "When will I get that money? Hmm? Hurry up, because the situation is really, really serious!"

"Calm down, Grandfather," I replied. "I found someone who's helping me."

"Good job!" he said gruffly.

I hung up and turned around.

Trap was already on my house phone, FRANTICALLY making calls.

"I have a house that's just right for you, Doctor Hurtmouse," he squeaked. "Please hold . . ."

Then, "Hi, Mrs. Busymouse! Guess what? I found the PERFECT home for you — it's a real gem! Please hold . . ."

Then, "Countess de Snobberella, what a pleasure to hear from you! I have a beautiful house that would be just the thing for your noble niece. Please hold . . ."

Then, "Mr. Gorgonzola, you'll never believe what just popped up. This little house is *exactly* what you asked for. Please hold . . ."

It looked like Trap had things under control, so I sat down in my **PAWCHAIR** next to my fireplace and gave a bit of food to my little fish, HANNIBAL. He peered at me **SADLY** from inside his fishbowl.

"I'm afraid we need to **move** soon," I tried to explain to him. "I don't know where you and I will live yet, but I'll look for another house *right away*."

Suddenly, Trap **pinched** my tail.

"**OUCH!**" I yelled.

"**Shhh!**" he whispered. "I might have a **buyer** for your little shack!"

He returned to the phone.

"Good day, miss," he said in a very **PROFESSIONAL** voice. "Yes, of course it's for sale. **YES, YES, YES!** I guarantee it! What? Is it available right away? Of course it is! As soon as you need it, we'll **kick out** the current owner. Yes, his name is Geronimo Stilton: G-e-r-o-n-i-m-o S-t-i-l-t-o-n. Yes, you understood correctly.

"He runs *The Rodent's Gazette*. When

did you say you NEED the house? In an HOUR? Okay, I'll clear it out immediately, but you'll need to pay in cash. RIGHT AWAY! Do we have a deal?"

I was stunned. I tried to interrupt him to say that I couldn't even THINK of moving within the hour. But he waved me away and whispered, "Am I the best problem solver in New Mouse City or what?"

What? An Hour?!

Trap continued squeaking a mile a minute to the mouse on the phone. Then he smiled as wide as a cat who just trapped a rat.

"Okay, it's a deal!" he said proudly. "You come with a SUITCASE full of money, and I'll make sure the current owner is gone. Yes, of course the sale includes all the furniture. Absolutely! I'll throw in everything except the antique cheese rind collection from the 1700s. The owner will be keeping that."

"Wait!" I shouted. "I care about my furniture, too, not just the cheese rinds! You can't ask me to leave everything behind!"

"Shh!" Trap hissed, shushing me. "Let me work!"

Then he turned back to the phone.

"Okay, see you in one hour. Good-bye!"

Then he hung up, his eyes sparkling.

"I sold your house in exactly THREE hours, EIGHT minutes, and twenty seconds," he bragged. "I'm good, huh? Grandfather will be very happy!"

Then he PUSHED me toward the door to my room.

"Now start packing!" he ordered. "You don't have much time. Come on, hurry up!"

"But I can't leave all this behind so *quickly*!" I protested.

GERONIMO'S PRECIOUS ANTIQUE CHEESE RIND COLLECTION

This collection is the result of many years of expensive research. These unique pieces of the rarest and stinkiest cheeses come from all over Mouse Island!

"Come on now, what do you need aside from a TOOTHBRUSH, toothpaste, and an extra pair of underwear?" Trap asked. "I mean, maybe you'll want to take a blanket for those extra-cold nights . . ."

I sighed. I usually curl up by my fireplace on extra-cold nights. But not anymore!

Hannibal peered out at me from his fishbowl with wide eyes, as if to say, "Glub, glub! Hurry up, Geronimo, an hour goes by very quickly!"

So I went to find my suitcase. Then I put a toothbrush, toothpaste, a change of underwear, and my FAVORITE blanket (knitted by my dear aunt Sweetfur) inside. Finally, I packed up my precious antique cheese rind collection while Trap timed me with his STOPWATCH.

"Hurry, Geronimo," Trap squeaked. "You

still have three minutes — well, two and a half . . . two . . . one and a half . . . one . . . thirty seconds . . .”

I grabbed Hannibal’s **fishbowl** and headed toward the door, shuffling my paws sadly as Trap **shoved** me from behind.

“There’s no need to **PUSH ME**,” I complained. “I can leave on my own.”

As I stepped outside, I suddenly had a realization.

"You never told me WHO bought the house!" I told Trap. "Who is it?"

Trap backed away from me, shrugging his shoulders.

"Well, I didn't tell you because I can't," he explained. "This mouse bought the house on the CONDITION that you don't know who she — or he — is. Otherwise, no deal! Now go find someplace to SLEEP tonight! Don't worry — I'll collect the cash and bring it to Grandfather. Good-bye!"

And he slammed the door in my snout.

I stood in the street in front of my (well, not anymore!) house with Hannibal's fishbowl under my arm. I felt so sad and alone. The sun was setting and the air was getting colder and colder until a freezing wind began to blow. Snow began to fall in large flakes, covering the ground with a soft white carpet.

"Poor Hannibal!" I exclaimed, looking down at my pet fish. His fins were shivering in the chilly air. "I'd better find a hotel room before you freeze!"

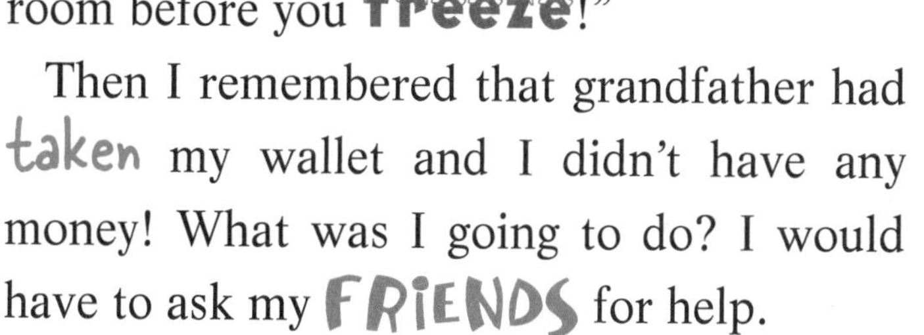

Then I remembered that grandfather had taken my wallet and I didn't have any money! What was I going to do? I would have to ask my FRIENDS for help.

So I took out my phone and began making calls. Unfortunately, no one was home. **Strange!** I tried everyone's cell phones, too, but no one answered. How very strange!

Suddenly, I remembered what day it was. Tomorrow was a New Mouse City holiday. All of my FRIENDS and relatives had left to go on vacation in the mountains! Only Trap and Grandfather had stayed in the city.

I remembered quite well, because I was the one who had organized the vacation (and PAID for the whole thing) just a few days earlier!

I had chosen an isolated, remote location where there was no cell phone reception because I wanted to spend a few days with my friends and family without ANYONE disturbing me with work! I was supposed to meet them there that evening.

I really didn't want to ask Trap for more HELP: He had already done so much for me. And I didn't want to ask my grandfather for HELP, either: He had a way of making every problem I had seem like it was entirely my fault! I decided I would find a place to stay on my own, like a REAL mouse.

I wandered around the city for hours,

trying to come up with a plan. Just as I was about to give up hope, I found myself near a small green space by the botanical gardens called Parmesan Park. I knew the spot well: I used to go there as a young mouse with Aunt Sweetfur!

I entered the park and walked down the path that used to lead to a small playground. There it was! The playground was still there. There was a slide, a seesaw, and even a small WOODEN house, where I had often played with my sister, Thea. It was all very run-down, but I had such fond memories of that little spot.

I hurried inside the tiny house, out of the snow and WIND. Then I curled up on the ground, hugging HANNIBAL'S fishbowl as I drifted off to sleep, the snow falling silently outside.

Zzzzz . . .
zzzzz

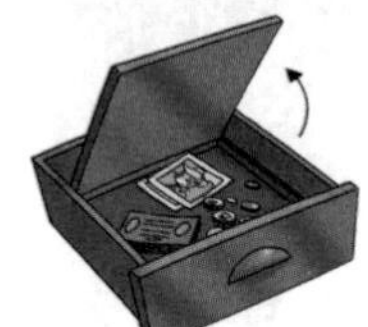

The Secret Drawer in My Desk

The next morning, I awoke at dawn because of the honking of the geese in the pond. The ground outside the little house was covered in a beautiful carpet of sparkling snow . . . how lovely! Other than the geese, there wasn't a soul around, and for a moment, I felt like the happiest and richest mouse in the world. But then I remembered that I had a SERIOUS problem to solve. I needed to find a new home for myself and Hannibal!

I hid my suitcase in a corner of the little house and headed to my office on foot, carrying Hannibal. I didn't have my wallet or any money, so I couldn't PAY to take a taxi, bus, or subway.

"*Geronimo*!" my coworkers greeted me, looking worried. "Is everything okay? You look so **disheveled**! Are you feeling **all right**?"

I didn't want anyone to know that I had slept in the playground, **curled up** in a tiny wooden house. And I didn't want anyone to **worry** about me. So I put on my best snout.

"I'm **f-fine**!" I stuttered, turning red. "Umm, I'm **great** — I mean, I'm okay, given the situation. I can't

COMPLAIN, even if things really could be **better**!"

I headed straight to the bathroom, where I tidied myself up. I really didn't want my coworkers to be worried about me.

I closed myself in my office and called the **BANK** right away. The bank manager, **Ledger Moneymouse**, answered the phone.

"Good morning, this is Geronimo Stilton," I began. "I need to come in right away to withdraw some money from my account."

Ledger began to SQUEAK back, but his voice sounded STRANGE — not at all like it usually does.

"I'm very sorry, Mr. Stilton, but that won't be possible," he told me.

"But why not?" I asked in surprise.

"Yesterday your grandfather stopped by and took out ALL your money," he replied. "He said you two had an agreement! He even showed me a piece of paper you signed. He said the money was for something important, maybe for *The Rodent's Gazette*?"

I turned as PALE as mozzarella as I remembered the sheet that my grandfather had made me sign.

Then I said good-bye and hung up the phone.

Holey Swiss cheese! The situation

It's better than nothing!

was more **serious** than I had imagined. I absolutely had to find another place to live, but I had very little **money**! All I had left were a few dollars that I had hidden in the bottom of my desk drawer in case of an emergency. You never knew when something **UNEXPECTED** might happen! (But, **SHHH**! Please don't tell anyone about it . . . it's a *secret*!)

I never thought I'd have to use it, but this really was an **EMERGENCY**!

I counted the money. It wasn't much, but it was better than **nothing**.

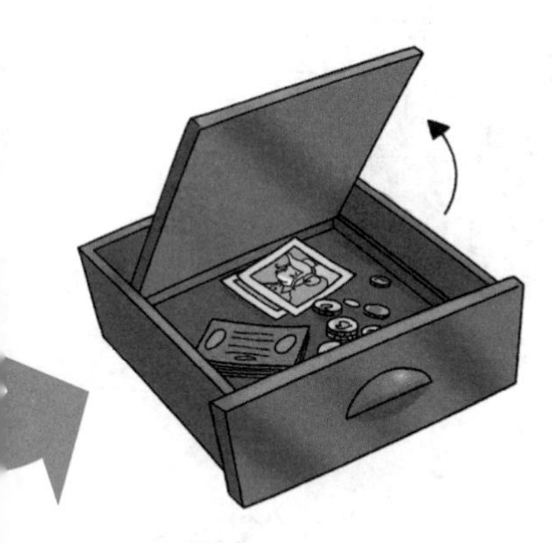

SECRET EMERGENCY CASH HIDDEN IN THE BOTTOM DRAWER OF MY DESK

House Hunting Begins

I needed to begin my house hunt, so I turned on the computer and went to the MouseHouse website.

As I scrolled through listings for apartments, condos, and houses, I thought about how I needed someone who specialized in solving DIFFICULT problems.

Wouldn't you know it, a second later, an intriguing ad POPPED UP on my screen. It was for a company called PROBLEM SOLVERS. The ad said they "solved problems of all kinds, from A to Z: from alligator attacks to zit-covered zebras!"

EXPERIENCE! EFFICIENCY! PROFESSIONALISM!
Do you have a problem that is small, medium, large, or enormouse?

LET US HANDLE IT!

It doesn't matter how much money you have — call us!
There's a solution for every problem, and we will find it (sooner or later)!
We're so sure we can solve your problem, we'll give you your money back if we don't succeed!

It seemed like the perfect solution. The ad even said it didn't matter how much money I had. How fabumouse!

Full of hope, I picked up the phone and dialed the PROBLEM SOLVERS.

"Heeeeello!" answered a male voice. "Problem Solvers! What's your problem?"

I couldn't place it, but the voice sounded very familiar.

"Well, I'm looking for a new place to live, but I'm a bit SHORT on cash," I explained.

"Don't worry about it!" the voice replied. "I can fix that for you! That's why I'm called the Problem Solver!"

How did I know that VOICE? It really seemed so familiar to me . . .

"I'll fix that for you **right away**—as QUICK as can be! Just yesterday I fixed an enormouse problem in just three hours, eight minutes, and twenty seconds . . ."

Holey cheese! That sounded like something I had heard before. But **WHO** was it on the other end of the phone?

"Let's meet in front of my office," he

continued. "The address is eleven Brie Boulevard."

I walked there right away, and when I arrived, the door burst open and a **chubby** rodent came out. He was wearing a yellow shirt with palm trees on it, and he had an earring in his left ear.

"**YOU** again?" he yelled.

"**YOU** again?" I replied with a groan.

CHEESE AND CRACKERS! It was my cousin Trap, of course!

"So you were the **mouse** on the phone!" he said with a chuckle. "I thought it sounded like you. Don't worry, I'll give you a **special** price! Now hop into my car and I'll show you **EVERYTHING** for sale here in New Mouse City and the surrounding areas."

He showed me the following:

A) an **ancient castle** with museumlike furniture and solid gold faucets . . .

B) a MODERN APARTMENT downtown

A LUXURIOUS ANCIENT CASTLE . . .

A MODERN APARTMENT DOWNTOWN . . .

designed by famouse architects . . .

C) a **nice house** in the suburbs that seemed cute and cozy, and . . .

D) a *simple little cottage* outside the city, in the middle of some farms.

Each time Trap told me the price I would begin to sob. Everything was much ***too expensive***!

Finally, he showed me a shabby shack with a drippy roof and a view of a toilet factory. It was right near a **construction** site, and the constant sound of jackhammers was deafening. Plus it smelled **terrible**

A NICE HOUSE IN THE SUBURBS . . .

A SIMPLE LITTLE COTTAGE IN THE COUNTRYSIDE . . .

A SHABBY SHACK . . .

because it was next to a nature preserve specifically for **skunks**!

I was sure I'd be able to afford the shack, but I was **wrong**. It was still **TOO EXPENSIVE**!

"What a **DIFFICULT** client you are!" Trap grumbled. "But I do have one more place . . ."

Would you believe it? He led me right to that little house in the playground in **Parmesan Park**!

"Here you go," he exclaimed **proudly**. "A house that's **free** to stay in! Am I the best **problem solver** in New Mouse City or what?"

My whiskers drooped in defeat.

"Can't you at least be **GRATEFUL**?" Trap grumbled.

I didn't want him to feel bad, so I didn't tell him that I had already discovered the little house the **NIGHT** before.

"Um, thanks," I squeaked. "This will be just fine for now."

As I settled in again to my **TEMPORARY** home, I made a plan. As soon as my friends and relatives returned from vacation, I would ask for their **help**!

THIS IS HOW I ORGANIZED THE LITTLE WOODEN HOUSE IN PARMESAN PARK!
2
9
6
7
3
8

KEY

1. MATTRESS MADE OF DRIED OAK LEAVES (THE SOFTEST MATERIAL FOR WHEN IT'S VERY COLD!)

2. BRAIDED WILLOW CURTAINS, SO THE WIND DOESN'T COME IN!

3. A SIMPLE CARDBOARD-BOX NIGHTSTAND

4. PINE RESIN TO SHINE MY WHISKERS

5. A MAPLE BRANCH TO COMB MY FUR

6. STORAGE SPOT FOR HANNIBAL'S FOOD

7. CAMPING PANS AND PLATES FOR MEALS

8. UPSIDE-DOWN PLANTER TO USE AS A STOOL

9. FIREPLACE FOR COOKING AND KEEPING WARM

10. PHOTOS OF BENJAMIN AND THEA SO I'D FEEL MORE AT HOME!

It's Party Time!

The next morning, I washed my whiskers in the park's fountain, **BRUSHED** my fur really well, and headed to *The Rodent's Gazette*. I was ready to face a hard day of work. But when I entered the office I was speechless. It was like a big Party in there!

Everyone was laughing, joking, and toasting with cheddar smoothies.

My coworker Priscilla Prettywhiskers gave

me an **ENORMOUSE** hug.

"We're saved!" she squeaked happily. "The **crisis** at *The Rodent's Gazette* is over!"

"Really? But how is that **possible**?" I asked, stunned.

"It's simple," Grandfather Shortpaws explained. "The crisis is **OVER** because there never really was a crisis!"

"What do you mean, there was **NO CRISIS**?" I asked, my whiskers twisting in confusion.

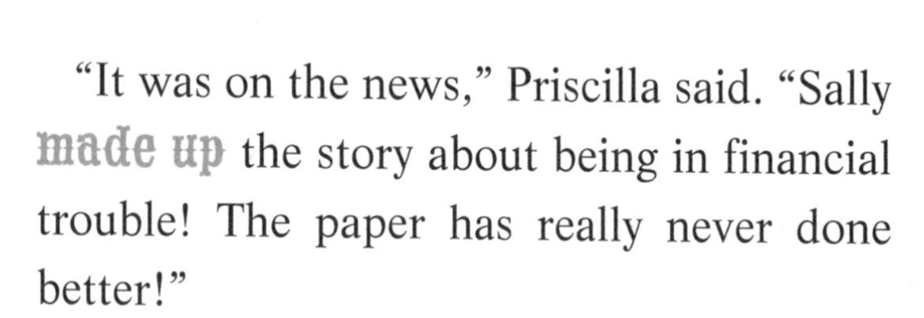

"It was on the news," Priscilla said. "Sally made up the story about being in financial trouble! The paper has really never done better!"

I turned on the television. The news reporter confirmed it: The crisis at *The Rodent's Gazette* had been a hoax. It wasn't **TRUE**! And Sally Ratmousen was denying any responsibility for the story.

A moment later, Sally appeared on the SCREEN in the fur.

"It's not my fault Ledger Moneymouse messed up the accounts, is it?" she squeaked defiantly. "So what if I ended up selling a few more copies of *The Daily Rat* as a result?"

What a dishonest rodent! That sly mouse had clearly invented the whole story to sell more copies of her **newspaper**. And because of her, I had to sell my *house*!

Grandfather clapped his paw on my shoulder sympathetically. Then he gave me back my GOLD watch, my PLATINUM pen, and my WALLET.

"Here you go, Grandson!" he boomed. "But don't spend all your money in one place. You **never know** what might happen in the future . . ."

"But, Grandfather, what about my house?" I asked in dismay. "What will I do now?"

"What do you mean?" he barked gruffly.

"Grandfather, I don't have a home," I reminded him impatiently. "REMEMBER? You made me **sell** it so that you could have some extra cash to **SAVE** the newspaper!"

"Oh, yes, yes, of course I remember," he mumbled under his whiskers. Honestly, I think he had FORGOTTEN!

"Well, there's no need for you to make sacrifices anymore, Grandson," he said. "I'll give back the money you gave me to save *The Rodent's Gazette*."

And he handed me a check.

I dashed out the door, calling, "Thanks! See you later! I have something very urgent to do!"

I ran right to Trap's new office. He was sitting at his desk with his paws up. When he saw me, he raised his eyebrow.

"You again?" he said. "What can I do for

you now, Cousin? More problems? Just tell me what you need and I'll handle it! I'm not one to brag, but I'm the best!"

I gasped, trying to catch my breath. I had just RUN as fast as I could all the way from *The Rodent's Gazette*!

"The CRISIS is over," I explained. "I mean, there never was a crisis! Grandfather gave me back my money, and now I want my house back."

Trap knocked on my head with his paw.

"Knock, knock! Anybody home?" he joked. "You forgot one minor detail, Cuz: When you sold your house, you sold it! There's nothing to be done. The only thing you can do is try to buy it back!"

"Then TELL ME who bought it!" I demanded.

He shook his head.

"No can do," he said stubbornly. "I promised the buyer I wouldn't tell."

He sat back in his chair. But as he spoke, I noticed that he shuffled some of the folders on his desk. He grabbed one and pushed it in front of me casually, as though it wasn't important.

I couldn't help seeing the writing on the front of the folder:

Buyer: Sally Ratmousen
Seller: Geronimo Stilton
Address: 8 Mouseford Lane

I immediately understood.

"Don't worry, you don't have to break your promise," I told him. "I get it!"

He winked at me. "Good luck, Cuz!"

In Sally Ratmousen's Lair

I headed to *The Daily Rat* to talk to Sally Ratmousen. She calls herself my "enemy number one," but I just refer to her as the editor of *The Rodent's Gazette*'s biggest competitor. She'll do whatever it takes to try to get ahead of my newspaper. And this time she almost destroyed *The Rodent's Gazette* for **GOOD**!

Sally is very, very **AMBITIOUS**. Sometimes I feel sorry for her because it really isn't **worth** it! There's room in New Mouse City for **TWO** newspapers and **TWO** opinions, but

Sally doesn't SEE it that way.

When I arrived at the offices of *The Daily Rat*, the newsroom staff was shocked to see me.

"*Geronimo Stilton?*" someone squeaked. "But aren't you the publisher of *The Rodent's Gazette*? What are you doing here?"

I ran up the stairs to Sally's office.

"No need to let her know I'm here!" I yelled. "I'll do it MYSELF!"

I entered Sally's office. It was HUGE, with elegant steel and glass furniture that sparkled in a SINISTER way. It may have been fancy, but it was cold and unwelcoming.

My office, on the other paw, was warm and inviting. It was furnished with antique furniture, books, and cozy lighting. It was SIMPLE but welcoming!

THE DAILY RAT
SALLY'S OFFICE

Sally was seated at a triangular glass table. She sneered when she saw me.

"Oh, hello, *Geronimo*," she said coldly. "What can I do for you?"

I **gulped**, trying to gather my courage.

"Um, well, I learned today that you are the **mouse** who bought my ***house*** . . ."

"That **sad** little shack?" she asked with a laugh. "That place is a real rat trap. Yes, I bought it. WHY?"

"Because I would like to **buy it back**!" I replied boldly.

She broke out in an enormouse laugh.

"Ha, ha, ha, ha, ha, ha! You want to **buy back** the house?" she asked, incredulous. "Don't even think about it! Do you have any IDEA what I plan to do with that house?"

"No," I whispered. "I don't."

My head was **spinning** with fear. What if Sally wouldn't sell my house back to me? I grabbed the edge of the desk to **STEADY** myself.

She **WAVED** my house keys in front of my snout.

"Your house will be **knocked down**

and destroyed to make way for something new and AMAZING!"

She wagged her finger at me, delighting in my shocked expression.

"What would you rather, Geronimo?" she taunted me. "A fish food factory? A gloomy cemetery? Or maybe a stinky landfill?"

My whiskers trembled at the thought of a fish food factory standing where my beautiful little house had been!

"Please, Sally," I begged, getting down on my knees. "Please sell MY HOUSE back. I'm lost without it! I left my heart in that house, and I would do anything to get it back!"

She snickered, happy to see me so humiliated.

"I'll give you your house back," she agreed

A FISH FOOD FACTORY . . .
A GLOOMY CEMETERY . . .
OR A STINKY LANDFILL!

SMOOTHLY. "But ONLY if the sun rises in the west instead of the EAST. Or if the color of the sea turns from blue to RED!"

She laughed again. Then she pointed to a poster on the wall behind her. It showed a tall and THIN rodent playing basketball.

"Or . . ." she began thoughtfully. "If you can get an interview with Bounce Ballmouse."

My jaw dropped. "You mean *that* Bounce Ballmouse?" I asked, pointing to the poster. "The extremely famouse basketball player? The one who is extra famouse because he has *never, ever, ever* given even ONE interview in his whole life?"

"Yes, that's the one!" Sally said smugly. "If you can get an interview with him in the next twelve hours, I'll give your house back, and you can even keep my MONEY!

"But if **YOU LOSE**," Sally continued. "I will keep your house. And you will work for me for the rest of your life . . . for **FREE**!"

FIRST NAME: Bounce
LAST NAME: Ballmouse
WHO HE IS: A super-famouse basketball player.
HIS PASSION: Basketball! But he also loves to read, listen to classical music, and cook.
HIS SECRET DREAM: To play (and win!) the game of the century against the Catburg Lakers.
HIS MOTTO: A game a day keeps the doctor away.

Bounce, Bounce, Bounce!

What a challenge! I was very worried. The chances of me getting an interview with Bounce were terrible! But I had to at least try. I wanted to go HOME to my cozy, warm mouse hole, so I had to get that interview.

"I'll do it!" I told Sally.

She grabbed a stopwatch.

"Okay, you have exactly twelve hours," she ordered me. "That's until ten tonight!"

I ran outside, stopping by my office to drop off HANNIBAL. Then I headed toward Bounce Ballmouse's house: It was a super-luxurious villa at the top of a hill on the edge of the city.

I thought of all I knew about Bounce: He was **very tall**, very good at playing basketball, and he held the **RECORD** for the most baskets ever scored on Mouse Island. But I didn't know anything about his childhood or his family because he had never given an interview!

The odds were DEFINITELY against me, but I had less than twelve hours to make an interview happen.

So I positioned myself in front of his house with a notebook in my paw, and waited for my CHANCE.

Finally, his car drove through the gates.

"Mr. Ballmouse!" I shouted. "May I please have an interview?"

The car WHIZZED by without even stopping.

I heaved a big sigh. I'd just have to wait until he got back.

Later that afternoon, Bounce returned to his house on foot, surrounded by **BODYGUARDS**. They were all carrying lots of shopping bags, but they still looked **THREATENING**.

I tried to approach Bounce, but one of the bodyguards **STEPPED** in front of me.

"Please back away," he said seriously. "Do not disturb Mr. Ballmouse. He doesn't give

interviews — **ever**!"

That fact was becoming painfully clear to me. What was I going to do?! The twelve hours were almost up. If I failed, not only would I not get my **house** back but I would also have to work for Sally for the *rest of my life*!

It was getting DARK, and I was starting to lose hope. Suddenly, the gates

opened again — and Bounce Ballmouse came out!

I **ran** up to him.

"I beg you, Mr. Ballmouse," I asked desperately. "May I **please** have an interview?"

He **jogged** right past me without even stopping, dribbling a basketball to the **RHYTHM** of his steps.

His guards ran along with him. I ran after them, trying to **KEEP UP**, but they were all *so fast*!

Now I knew why he was the most **famouse** basketball player on Mouse Island: He was in exceptional shape! He ran like a **train** that never slowed or stopped. I was left far behind.

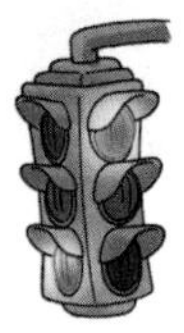

Bounce Ballmouse's Secret

I was about to turn back when the **unthinkable** happened. I noticed an old lady rodent at the corner of the street. She was about to cross, but she wasn't in the **CROSSWALK** — and headed straight for her was an **ENORMOUSE** truck whose driver wasn't paying attention to what he was doing!

She stepped off the sidewalk and into the street.

"**STOOOOOOOOP!**" I shouted as I raced toward her.

Luckily, she heard me and stopped. The truck swerved around her.

Unluckily for me, I **TRIPPED** on the

HOTEL
Stooooooooop!

sidewalk, HIT my head on the asphalt, and fainted.

A moment later, I came to.

"M-ma'am, are you okay?" I asked the rodent.

She looked at me gratefully.

"Thank you, young mouse," she squeaked. "You saved me!"

The truck driver ran up to us.

"I'm so sorry," he said seriously. "I didn't see you there!"

"It's okay," she said with a smile. "This rodent came by at just the right moment."

"At your service," I said, kissing her paw.

"You are a true GENTLEMOUSE," she said gratefully. "Your kind doesn't exist anymore!"

I turned as RED as a tomato. You see, I'm really very shy! I was about to turn to leave when I heard a voice call out: "Mom!"

I turned to see a mouse running toward us. It was none other than Bounce Ballmouse!

He hugged the old rodent tightly.

"Are you all right, Mom?" he asked, worried.

"Don't worry, BOUNCY, everything is okay," she squeaked softly to her son. "This kind young rodent saved my life!"

Bounce turned toward me and shook my paw gratefully.

"How can I ever THANK YOU?" he asked.

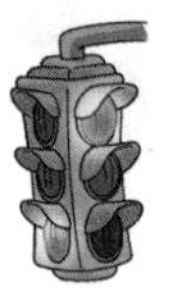

"I will give you anything you want!"

"Well, there is one thing I could really use," I replied EXCITEDLY. "Allow me to introduce myself. My name is Stilton, *Geronimo Stilton*. I'm the publisher of *The Rodent's Gazette*."

He gave me a friendly smile.

"That's my favorite **newspaper**. I read it every morning!" he replied.

"Well, the thing is . . ." I began.

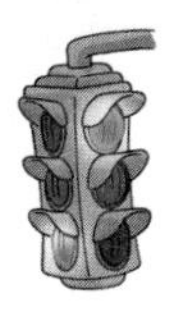

"Say no more!" Bounce said with a chuckle. "You want an interview, don't you? Well, please join me for dinner, and I will **happily** give you an interview! I'll tell you a secret: I've never given an interview before because I'm really VERY SHY! But I'll make an exception for you, because I can tell you're a rodent with **good intentions**, especially after what **HAPPENED** today!"

"I'm also very shy," I **confessed**. "So I truly understand!"

When he heard that, we **LAUGHED** together. As we headed back to his house, we shared stories about all the times that we *stammered* and blushed for no reason. As I interviewed him, I learned we had a lot of other things in common, too.

We both shared a passion for **reading** and for **classical music**, for example! And I

BOUNCE AS A BABY WITH HIS MOM

discovered that he had a little GOLDFISH for a pet, too. Her name was Charlotte, and I couldn't WAIT to introduce her to Hannibal!

BOUNCE AND HIS FISH, CHARLOTTE

Bounce's mom was an **excellent** cook, and prepared ***incredibly*** tasty cheese for us. Then Bounce showed me all his **trophies** and awards, and told me stories about his childhood.

EATING DINNER WITH BOUNCE AND HIS MOM

When I told him that I was really uncoordinated when it came to sports, he took me to his private **basketball** court and **taught** me how to shoot a basket! By the end of the evening, it felt as though we had known each other forever.

It was almost ten o'clock when I looked down at my **WATCH**.

"Oops!" I squeaked. "I'm sorry, but I have to go, or I'll lose my house!"

I hurried to Sally's office with the notes and *photos* from my fabumouse interview.

I was thrilled not only to have gotten the interview but also to have made an incredible **NEW FRIEND**!

BOUNCE PLAYING BASKETBALL AS A YOUNG MOUSE

BOUNCE WITH HIS TROPHIES

A LESSON FROM A CHAMPION

Now Give Me Back My House!

I checked the time: I had just **ten minutes** to **GET BACK** to Sally and win back my house! I reached *The Daily Rat* with only **three** minutes to spare . . .

I saw that Sally's office was lit up. She was waiting for me! I ran inside, breathless, just as the stopwatch went off. **Beep! Beep!**

Before I could squeak, Sally waved the keys to my house in front of my snout.

"So, Stilton, do you give up?" she taunted me. "It was impossible to interview Bounce Ballmouse, wasn't it? I was sure it would be, or I never would have given you the chance to get your house back for free!"

She threw back her snout and laughed.

"Ha, ha, ha, haaa! Are you prepared to work for me for the rest of your life?"

Once she was done squeaking, I could finally get a word in. I PROUDLY pulled from my jacket pocket the notebook with the interview.

"You'll be surprised to know, Sally, that Bounce DID give me the interview," I said calmly.

Her jaw hit the floor.

"Bounce Ballmouse?" she asked, incredulous.

"An interview? I don't believe you!"

So I pulled out my camera and showed her the **PHOTOS** I had taken with Bounce.

Before she could squeak another word, Sally **FAINTED**. Her colleagues had to **wake her up** by waving some aged cheese under her snout.

"S-so, that's it . . . you win," she stammered. "I must give you back your **HOUSE**, and you'll even get to keep my **money**."

"Exactly, Sally," I agreed.

"But that's not fair!" she howled.

"It *is* fair, Sally," I replied decisively. "You proposed the challenge, and I won! So please give me the KEYS."

She handed me the keys halfheartedly, and I raced out of the offices of *The Daily Rat*, my HEART full of happiness. I had my home back!

On my way home, I passed by the house of Ledger Moneymouse, the manager of Ratley's Bank.

I've known Ledger for many years, which is why I thought it was okay to stop by his house at that time of night.

"I'm SO sorry for the

misunderstanding, Mr. Stilton!" he said as soon as he saw me. "Please tell your grandfather how bad I feel about the mistake. He's been a client of ours for so long! You see, someone — I don't know who! — locked me in the bank's broom closet and took my place at the bank for a day. Then that person spread those false rumors about *The Rodent's Gazette*! As soon as I got out of the closet, I called the TV station and explained that there was no financial crisis at your newspaper. But I couldn't tell them that someone came into the BANK and managed to lock me up, now could I? I'm sure you understand how bad that would make the bank look. We have to maintain our reputation! Please don't tell anyone what happened!"

"Don't worry. I won't reveal your secret,"

I reassured him.

Then he showed me the rubber **mask** and some clothes that were identical to his that he'd found at the bank.

"Look at these!" he exclaimed. "Whoever impersonated me is certainly very *envious* of the success of your newspaper. I have an IDEA or two about who it might have been . . . Do you?"

I was pretty certain I knew exactly who it had been, but I didn't have any **proof**!

THE REAL LEDGER MONEYMOUSE

SALLY RATMOUSEN DRESSED AS LEDGER MONEYMOUSE

Welcome Back, Mr. Stilton!

Since everything had been cleared up, I said good-bye to **LEDGER** and headed to *The Rodent's Gazette* to get HANNIBAL. He and I could finally go **home**!

When I left my house the next morning, my

neighbors all crowded around me, hugging me.

"Welcome home, Mr. Stilton! We missed you so much!"

As soon as I got to *The Rodent's Gazette,* all of my colleagues stopped by my office to celebrate as well.

"We heard the news, Geronimo!" Priscilla said. "Thanks for everything you did for us. You're a real mouse . . . no, a real HERO!"

Then they carried me triumphantly around the office.

When my friends and FAMiLY heard what happened, they became upset.

"Why didn't you ask for our help, Geronimo?" my sister, Thea, asked.

"Yeah, Uncle G!" my nephew Benjamin agreed. "We would have been there for you!"

"I knew I could count on you," I replied,

moved at their generosity. "But when I tried to call you, no one answered their phones! *You were all on vacation!*"

"I was here, though!" Trap **BOASTED**, stepping forward. "And I helped you! But are you even grateful?"

I HUGGED him tightly.

"Of course I am, Trap!" I said. "And to

show you my gratitude, you're invited to my house for a fabumouse dinner. In fact, everyone is invited! Now that it's my house again, we must have a party to celebrate!"

And that is how this adventure ends — with a delicious dinner of DELECTABLE cheeses, the company of dear friends, and lots and lots of joy and happiness!

As I was cleaning up after dinner, I felt truly content.

Cheese niblets! I thought. *This really is a happy ending!*

Later that night, I lay in my nice, warm bed with the covers pulled way up to my snout and HANNIBAL'S fishbowl on the nightstand beside me. I thought about the money Sally had paid for the house. What would I do with it? It was quite a bit of money! I thought long and hard, because I wanted to make good use of it.

I remembered that when I had been without a home, there was a special place in New Mouse City where I had found some WARMTH and COMFORT. It was in PARMESAN PARK! How I would love to restore the park to its former SPLENDOR!

I also thought of all the rodents in New Mouse City who weren't lucky enough to have their own homes. What if I used part of the money to restore Parmesan Park, and the rest to build a lovely, affordable residence for rodents who were down on their luck?

So that's exactly what I did. By spring, Parmesan Park had newly planted trees, flowers, and flower beds; a modern

irrigation system; and newly restored FOUNTAINS, bridges, and pathways. It was more BEAUTIFUL than ever!

It was wonderful to see young mouselets playing between the flower beds and on the slides and SEESAWS. I was also delighted to see them playing in that cozy WOODEN house that had given me a place

of refuge on that cold winter's night!

I reflected on what had just happened to me. My most recent adventure had taught me that in life, it's important to react quickly, accept change, have faith in yourself, and never lose hope.

And above all else, it's essential to know how to ask your friends for help! I thought warmly about my family and all my friends — old and new — and how they are always ready to help me. And I also thought about all the FEARFUL, EXCITING, and mysterious adventures I've shared with them over the years. They've helped to shape who I am as a mouse. And I give you my word that this adventure won't be my LAST. Mouse's honor!

Be sure to read all my fabumouse adventures!

#1 Lost Treasure of the Emerald Eye

#2 The Curse of the Cheese Pyramid

#3 Cat and Mouse in a Haunted House

#4 I'm Too Fond of My Fur!

#5 Four Mice Deep in the Jungle

#6 Paws Off, Cheddarface!

#7 Red Pizzas for a Blue Count

#8 Attack of the Bandit Cats

#9 A Fabumouse Vacation for Geronimo

#10 All Because of a Cup of Coffee

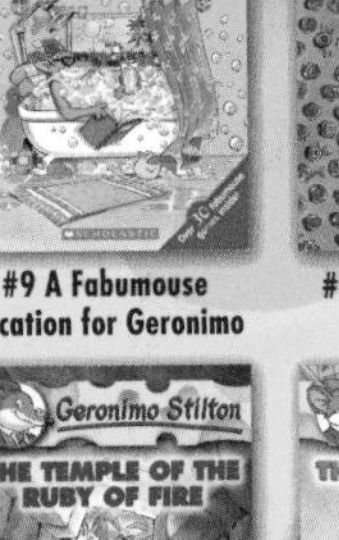

#11 It's Halloween, You 'Fraidy Mouse!

#12 Merry Christmas, Geronimo!

#13 The Phantom of the Subway

#14 The Temple of the Ruby of Fire

#15 The Mona Mousa Code

#16 A Cheese-Colored Camper

#17 Watch Your Whiskers, Stilton!

#18 Shipwreck on the Pirate Islands

#19 My Name Is Stilton, Geronimo Stilton

#20 Surf's Up, Geronimo!

#21 The Wild, Wild West

#22 The Secret of Cacklefur Castle

A Christmas Tale

#23 Valentine's Day Disaster

#24 Field Trip to Niagara Falls

#25 The Search for Sunken Treasure

#26 The Mummy with No Name

#27 The Christmas Toy Factory

#28 Wedding Crasher

#29 Down and Out Down Under

#30 The Mouse Island Marathon

#31 The Mysterious Cheese Thief

Christmas Catastrophe

#32 Valley of the Giant Skeletons

#33 Geronimo and the Gold Medal Mystery

#34 Geronimo Stilton, Secret Agent

#35 A Very Merry Christmas

#36 Geronimo's Valentine

#37 The Race Across America

#38 A Fabumouse School Adventure

#39 Singing Sensation

#40 The Karate Mouse

#41 Mighty Mount Kilimanjaro

#42 The Peculiar Pumpkin Thief

#43 I'm Not a Supermouse!

#44 The Giant Diamond Robbery

#45 Save the White Whale!

#46 The Haunted Castle

#47 Run for the Hills, Geronimo!

#48 The Mystery in Venice

#49 The Way of the Samurai

#50 This Hotel Is Haunted!

#51 The Enormouse Pearl Heist

#52 Mouse in Space!

#53 Rumble in the Jungle

#54 Get into Gear, Stilton!

#55 The Golden Statue Plot

#56 Flight of the Red Bandit

Special Edition!

The Hunt for the Golden Book

#57 The Stinky Cheese Vacation

#58 The Super Chef Contest

#59 Welcome to Moldy Manor

Special Edition!

The Hunt for the Curious Cheese

#60 The Treasure of Easter Island

#61 Mouse House Hunter

Up Next!

#62 Mouse Overboard!

Join me and my friends as we travel through time in these very special editions!

THE JOURNEY
HROUGH TIME

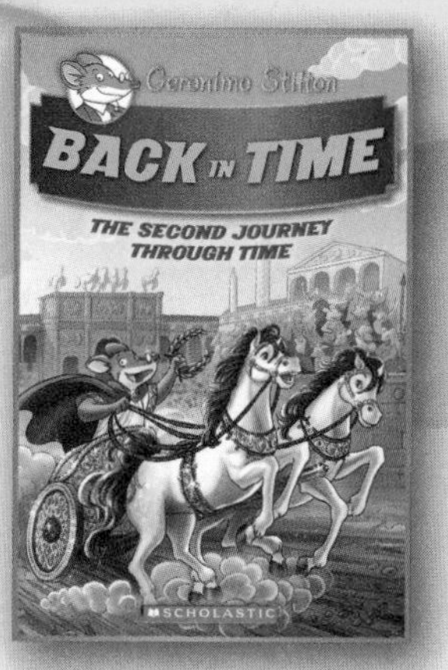

BACK IN TIME:
THE SECOND JOURNEY THROUGH TIME

THE RACE AGAINST TIME:
THE THIRD JOURNEY THROUGH TIME

Don't miss any of these exciting Thea Sisters adventures!

Thea Stilton and the Dragon's Code

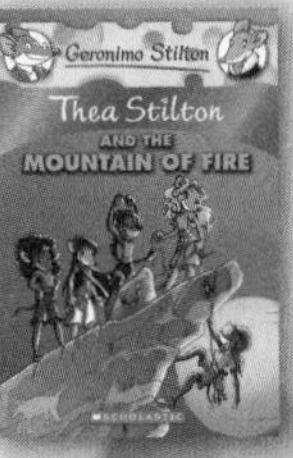

Thea Stilton and the Mountain of Fire

Thea Stilton and the Ghost of the Shipwreck

Thea Stilton and the Secret City

Thea Stilton and the Mystery in Paris

Thea Stilton and the Cherry Blossom Adventure

Thea Stilton and the Star Castaways

Thea Stilton: Big Trouble in the Big Apple

Thea Stilton and the Ice Treasure

Thea Stilton and the Secret of the Old Castle

Thea Stilton and the Blue Scarab Hunt

Thea Stilton and the Prince's Emerald

Thea Stilton and the Mystery on the Orient Express

Thea Stilton and the Dancing Shadows

Thea Stilton and the Legend of the Fire Flowers

Thea Stilton and the Spanish Dance Mission

Thea Stilton and the Journey to the Lion's Den

Thea Stilton and the Great Tulip Heist

Thea Stilton and the Chocolate Sabotage

Thea Stilton and the Missing Myth

Thea Stilton and the Lost Letters

Thea Stilton and the Tropical Treasure

Be sure to read all of our magical special edition adventures!

THE KINGDOM OF FANTASY

THE QUEST FOR PARADISE:
THE RETURN TO THE KINGDOM OF FANTASY

THE AMAZING VOYAGE:
THE THIRD ADVENTURE IN THE KINGDOM OF FANTASY

THE DRAGON PROPHECY:
THE FOURTH ADVENTURE IN THE KINGDOM OF FANTASY

THE VOLCANO OF FIRE:
THE FIFTH ADVENTURE IN THE KINGDOM OF FANTASY

THE SEARCH FOR TREASURE:
THE SIXTH ADVENTURE IN THE KINGDOM OF FANTASY

THE ENCHANTED CHARMS:
THE SEVENTH ADVENTURE IN THE KINGDOM OF FANTASY

THE PHOENIX OF DESTINY:
AN EPIC KINGDOM OF FANTASY ADVENTURE

THEA STILTON:
THE JOURNEY TO ATLANTIS

THEA STILTON:
THE SECRET OF THE FAIRIES

THEA STILTON:
THE SECRET OF THE SNOW

THEA STILTON:
THE CLOUD CASTLE

MEET GERONIMO STILTONIX

He is a spacemouse — the Geronimo Stilton of a parallel universe! He is captain of the spaceship *MouseStar 1*. While flying through the cosmos, he visits distant planets and meets crazy aliens. His adventures are out of this world!

#1 Alien Escape

#2 You're Mine, Captain!

#3 Ice Planet Adventure

#4 The Galactic Goal

#5 Rescue Rebellion

#6 The Underwater Planet

Meet GERONIMO STILTONOOT

He is a cavemouse — Geronimo Stilton's ancient ancestor! He runs the stone newspaper in the prehistoric village of Old Mouse City. From dealing with dinosaurs to dodging meteorites, his life in the Stone Age is full of adventure!

#1 The Stone of Fire

#2 Watch Your Tail!

#3 Help, I'm in Hot Lava!

#4 The Fast and the Frozen

#5 The Great Mouse Race

#6 Don't Wake the Dinosaur!

#7 I'm a Scaredy-Mouse!

#8 Surfing for Secrets

#9 Get the Scoop, Geronimo!

#10 My Autosaurus Will Win!

About the Author

Born in New Mouse City, Mouse Island, **Geronimo Stilton** is Rattus Emeritus of Mousomorphic Literature and of Neo-Ratonic Comparative Philosophy. For the past twenty years, he has been running *The Rodent's Gazette*, New Mouse City's most widely read daily newspaper.

Stilton was awarded the Ratitzer Prize for his scoops on *The Curse of the Cheese Pyramid* and *The Search for Sunken Treasure*. He has also received the Andersen 2000 Prize for Personality of the Year. One of his bestsellers won the 2002 eBook Award for world's best ratlings' electronic book. His works have been published all over the globe.

In his spare time, Mr. Stilton collects antique cheese rinds and plays golf. But what he most enjoys is telling stories to his nephew Benjamin.

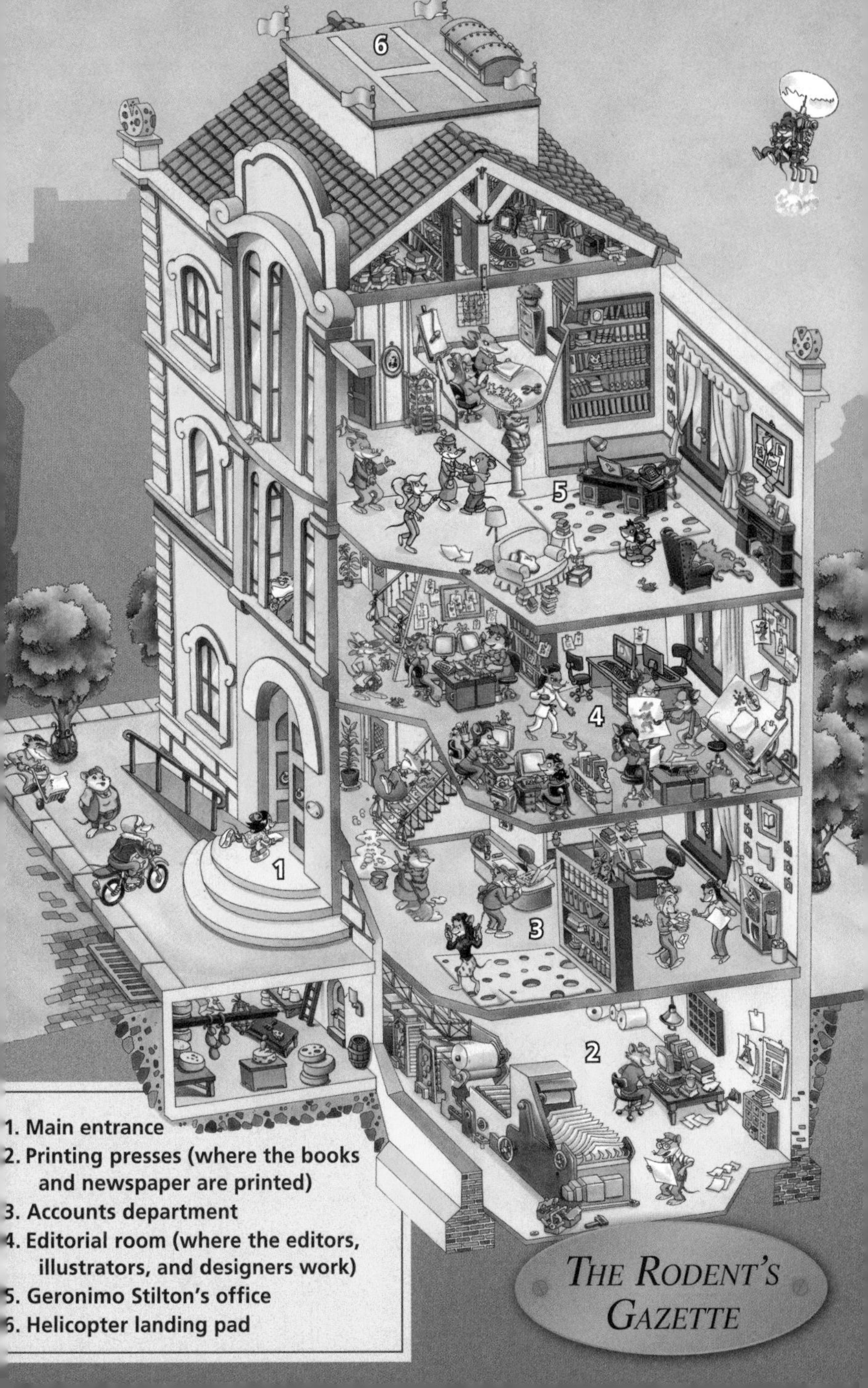

1. Main entrance
2. Printing presses (where the books and newspaper are printed)
3. Accounts department
4. Editorial room (where the editors, illustrators, and designers work)
5. Geronimo Stilton's office
6. Helicopter landing pad

THE RODENT'S GAZETTE

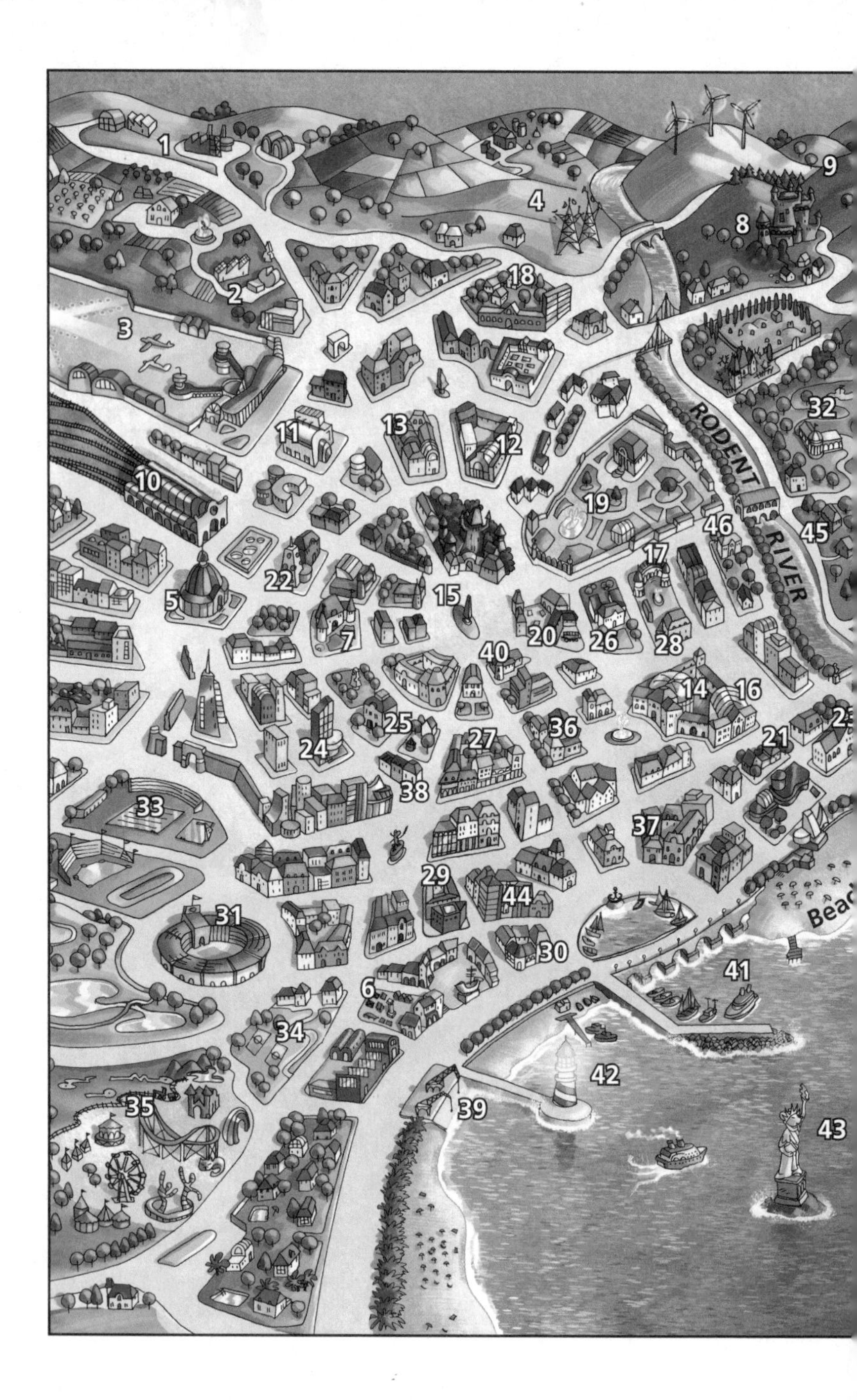
1
9
4
8
18
2
3
32
RODENT
RIVER
13
12
11
10
19
46
45
17
22
15
5
20
26
28
7
40
14
16
21
25
36
27
24
38
33
37
29
44
31
30
41
6
34
42
35
39
43

Map of New Mouse City

1. Industrial Zone
2. Cheese Factories
3. Angorat International Airport
4. WRAT Radio and Television Station
5. Cheese Market
6. Fish Market
7. Town Hall
8. Snotnose Castle
9. The Seven Hills of Mouse Island
10. Mouse Central Station
11. Trade Center
12. Movie Theater
13. Gym
14. Catnegie Hall
15. Singing Stone Plaza
16. The Gouda Theater
17. Grand Hotel
18. Mouse General Hospital
19. Botanical Gardens
20. Cheap Junk for Less (Trap's store)
21. Aunt Sweetfur and Benjamin's House
22. Mouseum of Modern Art
23. University and Library
24. *The Daily Rat*
25. *The Rodent's Gazette*
26. Trap's House
27. Fashion District
28. The Mouse House Restaurant
29. Environmental Protection Center
30. Harbor Office
31. Mousidon Square Garden
32. Golf Course
33. Swimming Pool
34. Tennis Courts
35. Curlyfur Island Amousement Park
36. Geronimo's House
37. Historic District
38. Public Library
39. Shipyard
40. Thea's House
41. New Mouse Harbor
42. Luna Lighthouse
43. The Statue of Liberty
44. Hercule Poirat's Office
45. Petunia Pretty Paws's House
46. Grandfather William's House

This way to the Rodent Straits
Brigand's Isle
Tomcat Island
Pirate Ship of Cats
Hamster Islands
Blue Dolphin Bay
Coral Reefs
This way to the Mousific Ocean
Stray Cat Harbor
Cat's Claw Bay
Panther Archipelago
Swissv
Cheddarton
Mouseport
San Mouscisco
This way to the Ratlantic Ocea
New Mouse City
Mousefort Beach
Furflung Island
N
W
E
S
MOUSE ISLAND
This way to the Sea of Mice
1
2
3
4
5
6
7
8
9
10
11
12
13
14
15
16
17
18
19
20
21
22
23
24
25
26
27
28
29
30
31
32
33
34
35
36
37

Map of Mouse Island

1. Big Ice Lake
2. Frozen Fur Peak
3. Slipperyslopes Glacier
4. Coldcreeps Peak
5. Ratzikistan
6. Transratania
7. Mount Vamp
8. Roastedrat Volcano
9. Brimstone Lake
10. Poopedcat Pass
11. Stinko Peak
12. Dark Forest
13. Vain Vampires Valley
14. Goose Bumps Gorge
15. The Shadow Line Pass
16. Penny Pincher Castle
17. Nature Reserve Park
18. Las Ratayas Marinas
19. Fossil Forest
20. Lake Lake
21. Lake Lakelake
22. Lake Lakelakelake
23. Cheddar Crag
24. Cannycat Castle
25. Valley of the Giant Sequoia
26. Cheddar Springs
27. Sulfurous Swamp
28. Old Reliable Geyser
29. Vole Vale
30. Ravingrat Ravine
31. Gnat Marshes
32. Munster Highlands
33. Mousehara Desert
34. Oasis of the Sweaty Camel
35. Cabbagehead Hill
36. Rattytrap Jungle
37. Rio Mosquito

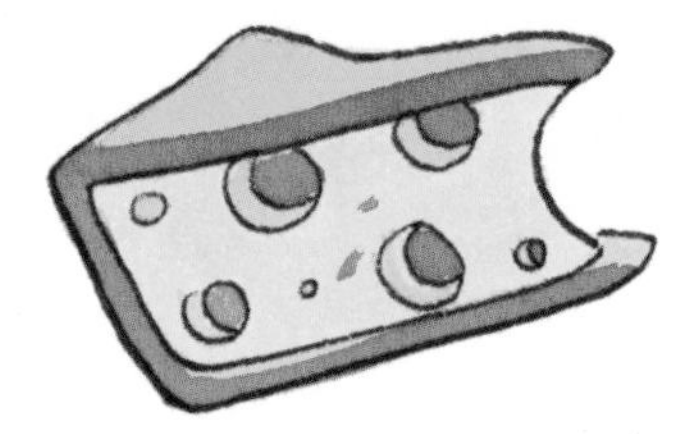

Dear mouse friends,
Thanks for reading, and farewell
till the next book.
It'll be another whisker-licking-good
adventure, and that's a promise!

Geronimo Stilton